ZAC
AND
EMILY

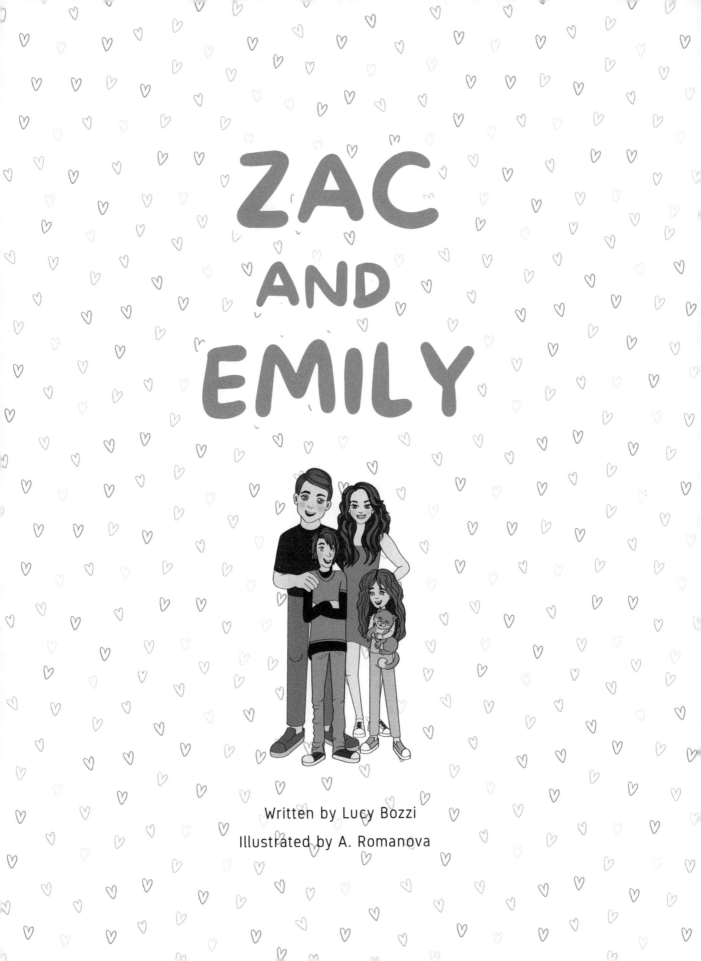

Written by Lucy Bozzi

Illustrated by A. Romanova

LUCY BOZZI
ZAC AND EMILY
POWER OF FAMILY

Illustrated by Alyona Romanova
Book Cover Design by Lucy Bozzi
Illustrations in this book were created by hand using Digital tools.
Typeset in A Day Without Sun.

This book is a work of fiction. Names, characters and scenes are either the product of the author's imagination or are used fictitiously, and any resemblance to actual persons, events of locales is entirely coincidental.

NUCLEAR FAMILY PUBLISHING

www.nuclearfamilypublishing.ca

Library and Archives Canada Cataloguing in Publication
ISBN 978-1-7389455-7-3

Happiness lies in the simplest moments spent with your loved ones

NUCLEAR FAMILY PUBLISHING

Main Characters

Zac

Emily

Kiki

Mom and Dad

"Zac!" "I'm so happy!"
Emily said proudly as she entered her brother's room.
"I passed my skating test!"
"My coach Ben said I did a beautiful spiral!"

"Figure skating is so boring, Emily!" said Zac.
"Hockey is way more fun!"
Zac looked away. He did not seem to be interested.
"And I love figure skating better!" said Emily.
"It's so beautiful!"

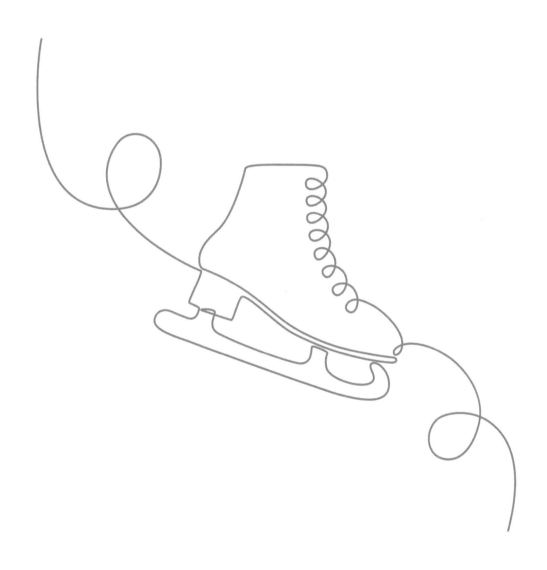

Zac and Emily live in Canada.

Zac plays hockey and is very good at scoring goals.

His hockey games are a lot of fun to watch.

Hockey is very popular in Canada.

Emily has been skating since she was two.
She loves practicing spirals and waltz jumps on ice.
Her dream is to become a professional figure skater.

Mom came into Zac's room.

"I am very proud of both of you!"

"Figure skating and hockey are both fun!"

"Why don't we head to the rink tomorrow?"

"You can show me some of your favorite moves on the ice."

Zac and Emily's Mom is a Doctor at the Children's Hospital.
She is very kind and caring. She loves yoga, and she bakes delicious
apple pies.

"Hey, kiddos!" chuckled Dad as he entered the house.
"I missed you guys so much!"
Zac and Emily ran to Dad throwing their arms around him in a big hug.
"We missed you too, Daddy!"

Zac and Emily's Dad is a design engineer.
He is smart and strong and
can fix anything in the house.

Every winter, Dad builds a skating rink in the backyard.

Everyone in the family loves skating.

Emily took Dad to the living room.
"Daddy, you can do many things!" said Emily.
"But there is one thing you can never do!"

"What is it, sweetie?" said Dad, wondering.

"You can't be our Mom!" giggled Emily.

"Indeed!" agreed Dad. "I can't argue with that!"

"Mom told me about your skating test!"

"Well done, sweetheart!"

"We shall celebrate!"

"I can't wait to show my spiral to you, Daddy!" said Emily.

As the family settled at the dinner table, Dad spoke up.
"When I was away from home on business last week,
I missed you all so much". "I feel so lucky to have you in my life!"

"I really missed playing baseball with you, Dad," said Zac.
"Don't go away for so long."

"And I missed reading books with you in the evening!" said Emily.

"We definitely missed you at dinner time," said Mom.
"No one likes when you are away."

24

"And Kiki missed you too!" added Mom, petting the cat gently.
Kiki purred happily.

"Mom and I have some exciting news to share!" said Dad at last.
"We are going on a family vacation!"

"We are flying to Europe!" said Dad. "All details tomorrow!"
"It's time to go to bed now!"

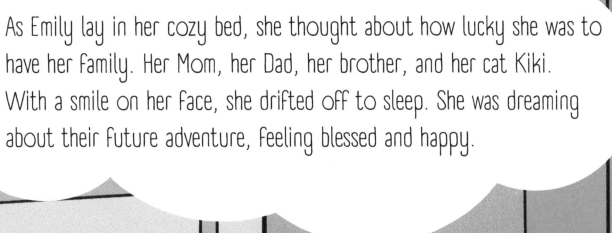

As Emily lay in her cozy bed, she thought about how lucky she was to have her family. Her Mom, her Dad, her brother, and her cat Kiki. With a smile on her face, she drifted off to sleep. She was dreaming about their future adventure, feeling blessed and happy.

NF Nuclear Family

NUCLEAR FAMILY PUBLISHING

31

Printed in the USA
CPSIA information can be obtained
at www.ICGtesting.com
JSHW070949190324
59269JS00003B/12

9 781738 945573